Hammatt Billings

Mother Goose for Grown Folks

A Christmas Reading

Hammatt Billings

Mother Goose for Grown Folks
A Christmas Reading

ISBN/EAN: 9783337163679

Printed in Europe, USA, Canada, Australia, Japan

Cover: Foto ©Andreas Hilbeck / pixelio.de

More available books at **www.hansebooks.com**

MOTHER GOOSE

FOR

GROWN FOLKS.

A CHRISTMAS READING.

ILLUSTRATED BY BILLINGS.

NEW YORK:

RUDD & CARLETON, 130 GRAND STREET.

(BROOKS BUILDING, CORNER OF BROADWAY).

M DCCC LX.

CONTENTS.

INTRODUCTORY.

SOMEWHERE in that uncertain "long ago,"
 Whose dim and vague chronology is all
That elfin tales or nursery fables know,
Rose a rare spirit, — keen, and quick, and
   quaint, —
Whom by the title, whether fact or feint,
 Mythic or real, Mother Goose we call.

Of Momus and Minerva sprang the birth
That gave the laughing oracle to earth:

1

A brimming bowl she bears, that, frothing
          high
     With sparkling nonsense, seemeth non-
          sense all;
Till, the bright, floating syllabub blown by,
Lo, in its ruby splendor doth upshine
The crimson radiance of Olympian wine
     By Pallas poured, in Jove's own banquet-
          hall.

The world was but a baby when she came;
So to her songs it listened, and her name
Grew to a word of power, her voice a spell
With charm to soothe its infant wearying
          well.
But, in a later and maturer age,
Developed to a dignity more sage,
Having its Shakspeares and its Words-
          worths now,

Its Southeys and its Tennysons, to wear

A halo on the high and lordly brow,

Or poet-laurels in the waving hair;

Its Lowells, Whittiers, Longfellows, to sing

Ballads of beauty, like the notes of spring,

The wise and prudent ones to nursery use

Leave the dear lyrics of old Mother Goose.

Wisdom of babes, — the nursery Shak-
    speare still, —

Cackles she ever with the same good-will:

Uttering deep counsels in a foolish guise,

That come as warnings, even to the wise;

As when, of old, the martial city slept,

Unconscious of the wily foe that crept

Under the midnight, till the alarm was heard

Out from the mouth of Rome's plebeian
    bird.

Full many a rare and subtile thing hath
  she,
Undreamed of in the world's philosophy :
Toss-balls for children hath she humbly
  rolled,
That shining jewels secretly enfold ;
Sibylline leaves she casteth on the air,
Twisted in fool's-caps, blown unheeded by,
That, in their lines grotesque, albeit, bear
Words of grave truth, and signal prophecy ;
And lurking satire, whose sharp lashes hit
A world of follies with their homely wit ;
With here and there a roughly uttered hint,
That makes you wonder at the beauty
  in't ;
As if, along the wayside's dusty edge,
A hot-house flower had blossomed in a
  hedge.

So, like brave Layard in old Nineveh,

Among the memories of ancient song,

As curious relics, I would fain bestir;

And gather, if it might be, into strong

And shapely show, some wealth of its

lost lore;

Fragments of Truth's own architecture,

strewed

In forms disjointed, whimsical, and rude,

That yet, to simpler vision, grandly stood

Complete, beneath the golden light of

yore!

BRAHMIC.

If a great poet think he sings,
   Or if the poem think it's sung,
They do but sport the scattered plumes
   That Mother Goose aside hath flung.

Far or forgot to me is near:
   Shakspeare and Punch are all the same;
The vanished thoughts do reappear,
   And shape themselves to fun or fame.

They use my *quills*, and leave me out,
   Oblivious that I wear the *wings*;

Or that a Goose has been about,
    When every little gosling sings.

Strong men may strive for grander thought,
    But, six times out of every seven,
My old philosophy hath taught
    All they can master this side heaven.

LITTLE BOY BLUE.

"Little boy blue! come blow your horn!
  The sheep in the meadow, the cows in the corn!
  Where's little boy blue, that looks after the sheep?
  He's under the hay-mow, fast asleep!"

Of morals in novels, we've had not a few;
With now and then novel moralities too;
And we've weekly exhortings from pulpit
      to pew;
But it strikes me, — and so it may chance
      to strike you, —
Scarce any are better than "Little Boy
      Blue."

For the veteran dame knows her business
    right well,
And her quaint admonitions unerringly
    tell:
She strings a few odd, careless words in a
    jingle,
And the sharp, latent truth fairly makes
    your ears tingle.

"Azure-robed Youth!" she cries, "up to
    thy post!
And watch, lest thy wealth be all scattered
    and lost:
Silly thoughts are astray, beyond call of
    the horn,
And passion breaks loose, and gets into the
    corn!

Is this the way Conscience looks after her
    sheep?
In the world's soothing shadow, gone sound-
    ly asleep?"

Is n't *that*, now, a sermon? No lengthened
    vexation
Of heads, and divisions, and argumenta-
    tion,
But a straightforward leap to the sure ap-
    plication;
And, though many a longer harangue is
    forgot,
Of which careful reporters take notes on
    the spot,
I think, — as the "Deacon" declared of his
    "shay,"

Put together for lasting for ever and aye, —
A like immortality holding in view,
The old lady's discourse will undoubtedly
"dew"!

JACK HORNER.

"Little Jack Horner
 Sat in a corner
Eating a Christmas Pie:
 He put in his thumb,
 And pulled out a plum,
And said, 'What a great boy am I!'"

Ah, the world hath many a Horner,
Who, seated in his corner,
Finds a Christmas Pie provided for his
 thumb:
And cries out with exultation,
When successful exploration
Doth discover the predestinated plum!

Little Jack outgrows his tire,
  And becometh John, Esquire;
And he finds a monstrous pasty ready made,
  Stuffed with notes and bonds and bales,
  With invoices and sales,
And all the mixed ingredients of Trade.

  And again it is his luck
  To be just in time to pluck,
By a clever " operation," from the pie
  An unexpected " plum";
  So he glorifies his thumb,
And says, proudly, " What a mighty man
      am I!"

  Or perchance, to Science turning,
  And with weary labor learning
All the formulas and phrases that oppress
      her, —

For the fruit of others' baking
So a fresh diploma taking,
Comes he forth, a full accredited Profes-
sor!

Or he's not too nice to mix
In the dish of politics;
And the dignity of office he puts on:
And he feels as big again
As a dozen nobler men,
While he writes himself the Honorable John!

Nay, he need not quite despair
Of the Presidential Chair:
The thing is not unlikely to be done;
Since a party puppet now
May wear boldly on its brow
The glory that a Webster never won!

Not to hint at female Horners,

　　Who, in their exclusive corners,

Think the world is only made of upper crust;

　　And in the funny pie

　　That we call Society,

Their dainty fingers delicately thrust:

　　Till it sometimes comes to pass,

　　In the spiced and sugared mass,

One may compass (don't they call it so?)

　　　　a *catch;*

　　And the gratulation given

　　Seems as if the very heaven

Had outdone itself in making such a match!

　　O, the world keeps Christmas Day

　　In a queer, perpetual way;

Shouting always, "What a great, big Boy

　　　　am I!"

Yet how many of the crowd,

Thus vociferating loud,

And its accidental honors lifting high,

Have really, more than Jack,

With all their lucky knack,

Had a finger in the *making* of the Pie?

2

BO–PEEP.

—————

> " Little Bo-Peep
>
>   Has lost her sheep,
>
> And does n't know where to find 'em;
>
>   Let 'em alone,
>
>   And they 'll come home,
>
> And bring their tails behind 'em."

Hope beckoned Youth, and bade him keep,
On Life's broad plain, his shining sheep,
And while along the sward they came,
He called them over, each by name;
This one was Friendship,— that was Health;
Another Love, — another Wealth;

One, fat, full-fleeced, was Social Station;
Another, stainless, Reputation;
In truth, a goodly flock of sheep, —
A goodly flock, but hard to keep.

Youth laid him down beside a fountain;
Hope spread his wings to scale a mountain;
And, somehow, Youth fell fast asleep,
And left his crook to tend the sheep:
No wonder, as the legend says,
They took to very crooked ways.

He woke — to hear a distant bleating, —
The faithless quadrupeds were fleeting!

Wealth vanished first, with stealthy tread,
Then Friendship followed — to be fed, —
And foolish Love was after led;

Fair Fame, — alas ! some thievish scamp
Had marked him with his own black stamp !
And he, with Honor at his heels,
Was out of sight across the fields.

Health just hangs doubtful, — distant Hope
Looks backward from the mountain slope, —
And Youth himself — no longer Youth —
Stands face to face with bitter Truth.

Yet let them go !   'T were all in vain
    To linger here in faith to find 'em ;
Forward ! — nor pause to think of pain, —
Till somewhere, on a nobler plain,
A surer Hope shall lead the train
Of joys withheld to come again
    With golden fleeces trailed behind 'em !

SOLOMON GRUNDY.

"Solomon Grundy
  Born on Monday,
  Christened on Tuesday,
  Married on Wednesday,
  Sick on Thursday,
  Worse on Friday,
  Dead on Saturday,
  Buried on Sunday:
  This was the end
  Of Solomon Grundy."

So sings the unpretentious Muse
That guides the quill of Mother Goose,
And in one week of mortal strife
Presents the epitome of Life:

But down sits Billy Shakspeare next,
And, coolly taking up the text,
His thought pursues the trail of mine,
And, lo! the "Seven Ages" shine!
O world! O critics! *can't* you see
How Shakspeare plagiarizes me?

And other bards will after come,
 To echo in a later age,
"He lived, — he died: behold the sum,
 The abstract of the historian's page";—
Yet once for all the thing was done,
 Complete in Grundy's pilgrimage.

For not a child upon the knee
But hath the moral learned of me;
And measured, in a seven days' span,
The whole experience of man.

BOWLS.

"Three wise men of Gotham
  Went to sea in a bowl:
  If the bowl had been stronger,
  My song had been longer."

MYSTERIOUSLY suggestive! A vague hint,
  Yet a rare touch of most effective art,
That of the bowl, and all the voyagers in 't,
  Tells nothing, save the fact that they did
    start.
There ending suddenly, with subtle craft,
The story stands, — as 't were a broken
    shaft, —

More eloquent in mute signification,
Than lengthened detail, or precise relation.
So perfect in its very non-achieving,
That, of a truth, I cannot help believing
A rash attempt at paraphrasing it
May prove a blunder, rather than a hit.

Still, I must wish the venerable soul
Had been explicit as regards the *bowl*.
Was it, perhaps, a railroad speculation?
Or a big ship to carry all creation,
That, by some kink of its machinery,
Failed, in the end, to carry even three?
Or other fond, erroneous calculation
Of splendid schemes that died disastrously?

It must have been of Gotham manufacture;
Though strangely weak, and liable to frac-
ture.

Yet — pause a moment — strangely, did I
    say ?

Scarcely, since, after all, it was but clay ; —

The stuff Hope takes to build her brittle
    boat,

And therein sets the wisest men afloat.

Truly, a bark would need be somewhat
    stronger,

To make the halting history much longer.

Doubtless, the good Dame did but gener-
    alize, —

Took a broad glance at human enterprise,

And earthly expectation, and so drew,

In pithy lines, a parable most true, —

Kindly to warn us ere we sail away,

With life's great venture, in an ark of
    clay,

Where shivered fragments all around be-
　　token,
How even the "golden bowl" at last lies
　　broken!

CRADLED IN GREEN.

"Rockaby, baby,
  Your cradle is green;
Father's a nobleman,
  Mother's a queen;
And Betty's a lady,
  And wears a gold ring,
And Johnny's a drummer,
  And drums for the king!"

O GOLDEN gift of childhood!
  That, with its kingly touch,
Transforms to more than royalty
  The thing it loveth much!

O second sight, bestowed alone
    Upon the baby seer,
That the glory held in Heaven's reserve
    Discerneth even here!

Though he be the humblest craftsman,
    No silk nor ermine piled
Could make the father seem a whit
    More noble to the child;
And the mother,—ah, what queenlier crown
    Could rest upon her brow,
Than the fair and gentle dignity
    It weareth to him now?

E'en the gilded ring that Michael
    For a penny fairing bought,
Is the seal of Betty's ladyhood
    To his untutored thought;

And the darling drum about his neck, -
  His very newest toy, —
A bandsman unto Majesty
  Hath straightway made the boy!

O golden gift of childhood!
  If the talisman might last,
How the dull Present still should gleam
  With the glory of the Past!
But the things of earth about us
  Fade and dwindle as we go,
And the long perspective of our life
  Is truth, and not a show!

"SIMILIA SIMILIBUS."

" There was a man in our town,
    And he was wondrous wise:
He jumped into a bramble-bush,
    And scratched out both his eyes.
But when he saw his eyes were out,
    With all his might and main
He jumped into another bush,
    And scratched them in again ! "

OLD Dr. Hahnemann read the tale,
    (And he was wondrous wise,)
Of the man who, in the bramble-bush,
    Had scratched out both his eyes.

And the fancy tickled mightily
   His misty German brain,
That, by jumping in another bush,
   He got them back again.

So he called it " homo-hop-athy " ·
   And soon it came about,
That a curious crowd among the thorns
   Was hopping in and out.
Yet, disguise it by the longest name
   They may, it is no use ;
For the world knows the discovery
   Was made by Mother Goose !

And not alone in medicine
   Doth the theory hold good :
In Life and in Philosophy,
   The maxim still hath stood :

A morsel more of anything,
   When one has got enough,
And Nature's energy disowns
   The whole unkindly stuff.

A second negative affirms;
   And two magnetic poles
Of charge identical, repel, —
   As sameness sunders souls.
Touched with a first, fresh suffering,
   All solace is despised;
But gathered sorrows grow serene,
   And grief is neutralized.

And he who, in the world's *mêlée*,
   Hath chanced the worse to catch,
May mend the matter, if he come
   Back, boldly, to the scratch;

Minding the lesson he received
　In boyhood, from his mother,
Whose cheery word, for many a bump,
　Was, Up and take another!

3

HOBBY-HORSES.

"I had a little pony,
  His name was Dapple Gray:
I lent him to a lady
  To ride a mile away.
She whipped him,
  She lashed him,
She rode him through the mire;
I would n't lend my pony now,
For all the lady's hire."

Our hobbies, of whatever sort
They be, mine honest friend,
Of fancy, enterprise, or thought,
'T is hardly wise to lend.

Some fair imagination, shrined
   In form poetic, maybe,
You fondly trusted to the World, —
   That most capricious Lady.

Or a high, romantic theory,
   Magnificently planned,
In flush of eager confidence
   You bade her take in hand.

But she whipped it, and she lashed it,
   And bespattered it with mire,
Till your very soul felt stained within,
   And scourged with stripes of fire.

Yet take this thought, and hold it fast,
   Ye Martyrs of To-day!
That same great World, with all its scorn,
   You've lifted on its way!

MISSIONS.

"Hogs in the garden,—
Catch 'em, Towser!
Cows in the cornfield,—
Run, boys, run!
Fire on the mountains,—
Run, boys, run boys!
Cats in the cream-pot,—
Run, girls, run!"

I DON'T stand up for Woman's Right;
Not I,—no, no!
The real lionesses fight,—
I let it go.

Yet, somehow, as I catch the call
 Of the world's voice,
That speaks a summons unto all
 Its girls and boys;

In such strange contrast still it rings
 As church-bells' bome
To the pert sound of tinkling things
 One hears at home;
And wakes an impulse, not germane
 Perhaps, to woman,
Yet with a thrill that makes it plain
 'T is truly human;—

A sudden tingle at the springs
 Of noble feeling,
The spirit-power for valiant things
 Clearly revealing.

But Eden's curse doth daily deal
 Its certain dole,—
And the old grasp upon the heel
 Holds back the soul!

So, when some rousing deed's to do,
 To save a nation,
Or, on the mountains, to subdue
 A conflagration,
Woman! the work is not for you;
 Mind your vocation!
Out from the cream-pot comes a mew
 Of tribulation!

Meekly the world's great exploits leave
 Unto your betters;
So bear the punishment of Eve,
 Spirit in fetters!

Only, the hidden fires will glow,
  And, now and then,
A beacon blazeth out below
  That startles men!

Some Joan, through battle-field to stake,
  Danger embracing;
Some Florence, for sweet mercy's sake
  Pestilence facing;
Whose holy valor vindicates
  The royal birth
That, for its crowning, only waits
  The end of earth;
And, haply, when we all stand freed,
  In strength immortal,
Such virgin-lamps the host shall lead
  Through heaven's portal!

GOING BACK TO OUR MUTTONS.

"There was an old man of Tobago,
Who lived on rice, gruel, and sago,
  Till, much to his bliss,
  His physician said this:
To a leg, sir, of mutton, you may go.
He set a monkey to baste the mutton,
And ten pounds of butter he put on."

"CHAIN up a child, and away he will go";
I have heard of the proverb interpreted so;
The spendthrift is son to the miser,—and
  still,
When the Devil would work his most piti-
  less will,

He sends forth the seven, for such embas-
  sies kept,
To the house that is empty and garnished
  and swept:
For poor human nature a pendulum seems,
That must constantly vibrate between two
  extremes.

The closer the arrow is drawn to the
  bow,
Once slipped from the string, all the further
  't will go:
Let a panic arise in the world of finance,
And the mad flight of Fashion be checked
  by the chance,
It certainly seems a most wonderful thing,
When the ropes are let go again, how it
  will swing!

And even the decent observance of Lent,

Stirs sometimes a doubt how the time has
　　been spent,

When Easter brings out the new bonnets
　　and gowns,

And a flood of gay colors o'erflows in the
　　towns.

So in all things the feast doth still follow
　　the fast,

And the force of the contrast gives zest to
　　the last;

And until he is tried, no frail mortal can
　　tell,

The inch being offered, he won't take the
　　ell.

We are righteously shocked at the follies
　　of fashion;

Nay, standing outside, may get quite in a
    passion
    At the prodigal flourishes other folks put
    on:
But many good people this side of Tobago,
If respited once from their diet of sago,
    Would outdo the monkey in basting the
    mutton!

GOING TO DOVER.

"Leg over leg
    As the dog went to Dover;
When he came to a stile,
    Jump he went over."

PERHAPS you would n't see it here,
But, to my fancy, 't is quite clear
That Mother Goose just meant to show
How the dog Patience on doth go:
With steadfast nozzle, pointing low, —
Leg over leg, however slow, —
And labored breath, but naught complaining,
Still, at each footstep, somewhat gaining, —

Quietly plodding, mile on mile,
    And gathering for a nervous bound
At every interposing stile,—
    So traversing the tedious ground,
Till all, at length, he measures over,
And walks, a victor, into Dover.

And, verily, no other way
Doth human progress win the day;
Step after step,—and o'er and o'er,—
Each seeming like the one before,
So that 't is only once a while,—
When sudden Genius springs the stile
That marks a section of the plain,
Beyond whose bound fresh fields again
Their widening stretch untrodden sweep,—
The world looks round to see the leap.

Pale Science, in her laboratory,
   Works on with crucible and wire
Unnoticed, till an instant glory
   Crowns some high issue, as with fire,
And men, with wondering eyes awide,
Gauge great Invention's giant stride.

No age, no race, no single soul,
By lofty tumbling gains the goal.
The steady pace it keeps between, —
The little points it makes unseen, —
By these, achieved in gathering might,
It moveth on, and out of sight,
And wins, through all that's overpast,
The city of its hopes at last.

RAGS AND ROBES.

" Hark, hark!

The dogs do bark;

Beggars are coming to town :

Some in rags,

Some in tags,

And some in velvet gowns!"

Coming, coming always!

Crowding into earth;

Seizing on this human life,

Beggars from the birth.

Some in patent penury;
　　Some, alas! in shame;
And some in fading velvet
　　Of hereditary fame;

But all in deep, appeaseless want,
　　As mendicants to live;
And go beseeching through the world,
　　For what the world may give.

Beggars, beggars, all of us!
　　Expectants from our youth:
With hands outstretched, and asking alms
　　Of Hope and Love and Truth.

Nor, verily, doth he escape
　　Who, wrapt in cold contempt,
Denies alike to give or take,
　　And dreams himself exempt;

Who never, in appeal to man,
  Nor in a prayer to Heaven,
Will own that aught he doth desire,
  Or ask that aught be given.

Whose human heart a stoic pride
  Folds as a velvet pall;
Yet hides a meagreness within,
  Worse beggary than all!

————

Coming, coming always!
  And the bluff Apostle waits
As the throng pours upward from the earth
  To Heaven's eternal gates.

In shreds of torn affection,
  In passion-rended rags;

4

While scarcely at the portal
     The great procession flags;

For the pillared doors of glory
     On their hinges hang awide;
Where each asking soul may enter,
     And at last be satisfied!

But a cold, calm shade arriveth,
     In self-complacent trim, —
And Peter riseth up to see
     Especially to him.

"Good morrow, saint! I'm going in
     To take a stroll, you know;
Not that *I want* for anything, —
     But just to see the show!"

"Hold!" thunders out the warden,
     "Be pleased to pause a bit!

For seats celestial, let me say,
    You 're not apparelled fit :
Yonder 's the brazen door that leads
    Spectators to the pit!

Whatever may be thought on earth,
    We 've other rules in heaven ;
And only poverty confessed
    Finds free admittance given !"

BLACKBIRDS.

"Sing a song o' sixpence, a pocket full of rye;
Four and twenty blackbirds baked in a pie:
When the pie was opened, they all began to sing,
And was n't this a dainty dish to set before the king?
The king was in his counting-house, counting out his
    money;
The queen was in the parlor, eating bread and honey;
The maid was in the garden, hanging out the clothes,
And along came a blackbird, and nipt off her nose!"

It does n't take a conjurer to see
The sort of curious pasty this might be;
A flock of flying rumors, caught alive,
And housed, like swarming bees within a
    hive, —

Instead of what were far more wisely
  done,
Having their worthless necks wrung, every
  one;—
And so a dish of dainty gossip making,
  Smooth covered with a show of secrecy,
That one but takes the pleasant pains of
  breaking,
  And out the wide-mouthed knaves pop,
  eagerly.

Blackbirds, indeed!   Each chattering *on-
  dit*
Comes forth, full feathered, black as black
  can be;
With quivering throats, all tremulous to
  sing,
And please, forsooth, some little social
  king;

Whose reign may last as long as he is able
To call his court around a dinner-table.

But, mark the sequel! When the laugh is
    over,
Think not to get the varlets under cover:
The crust once broken, you may seek in vain
To catch the birds, or coax them in again;
Mrs. Pandora's famous box, I wis,
Was nothing worse than such a pie as this:
And so, some pleasant morning, — when,
    down town,
  The king is busy with his bags of money,
Leaving at home the queenly Mrs. Brown
  Safe at her breakfast of fair bread and
    honey, —
Some quiet, harmless soul, who never
  knows
  Of any matters, save the plain pursuing

Her daily round,— the hanging out of
    clothes
Or other lawful work she may be doing, —
Finds, by the sudden nipping of her nose,
    What sort of mischief is about her brew-
        ing !

Not that, indeed, there 's anything to hinder
The thieves from flying though the parlor
    window ;
For never yet could sentinel or warden
Keep scandals wholly to the kitchen gar-
    den.

When, therefore, as not seldom it may be,
Even in the soberest community,
Strange revelations somehow get about, —
Like a mysterious cholera breaking out

Sudden, as Egypt's blains 'neath Aaron's rod,
Contagious by a whisper or a nod,—
When daily papers teem with many a hint
That daubs them darker even than their
　　　print;
When it would seem, in short, the very
　　　D——
Had let his little imps out on a spree;
Conclude, beyond a reasonable doubt,
Although, perhaps, you fail to trace it out,
Such plagues spring not unbidden from the
　　　ground,
And, if the thing were sifted, 't would be
　　　found
Somebody 's sown a pocket full of rye,
Or been regaling on a blackbird pie!

BANBURY CROSS.

" Ride a fine horse
   To Banbury Cross,
To see a young woman
   Jump on a white horse.
Rings on her fingers,
   And bells on her toes,
And she shall have music
   Wherever she goes."

PROPHETIC Dame! What hadst thou in thy
   view ?
A modern wedding in Fifth Avenue ?

Where,—like the goddess of a heathen
   shrine,
   With offerings heaped in such a glittering
     show
As must have emptied a Peruvian mine,
   And would suggest, but that we better
     know,
Marriage must be a bitter thing indeed,
   And, like the Prophet of the Eastern tale,
Must wear a very ugly face, to need
   Such careful shrouding in the silver
     veil,—
Her bridal pomp, as a white palfrey, mount-
     ing,
Caparisoned at cost beyond all counting,
With diamond-jewelled fingers, and the
     toes
Ditto, for all that anybody knows,

The smiling damsel goeth to the Banns?
  (Why add the "bury," or suggest the
    "cross,"
As if such brilliant ringing of the hands
  Preluded aught of trial or of loss?)

Shall not Life's golden bells still tinkle
    sweet,
And merry music make about her feet?
Shall not the silver sheen around her spread,
A lasting light along her pathway shed?

No mocking satire, surely, hides a sting,
  Nor bitter irony a truth foreshows,
In the gay chant the cheery dame doth
    sing, —
  "She shall have music wheresoe'er she
    goes"?

She shall have music !   Shall she sit apart,
  And let the folly-chimes outvoice the
    tone
That comes up wailing to the listening
    heart,
  From the great world, where misery
    maketh moan ?
Ah, Mother Goose ! if such the tale it tells,
Sing us no more your rhyme of rings and
    bells !

But may not — 't were a rare device in-
    deed ! —
The wondrous oracle in both ways read ?
And call up, as a fair beatitude,
The gracious vision of true womanhood,
That with pure purpose, and a gentle might,
Upheld and borne, as by the steed of white,

Pledged with her golden ring, goes nobly
    forth
To trace her path of joy along the earth, —
And, as she moves, makes music, silver-shod
" With preparation of the peace " of God,
That holds the key-note of celestial cheer,
And hangs heaven's echoes round her foot-
    steps here ?

THE MAD HORSE.

    " There was a mad man,
        And he had a mad wife,
    And the children were mad beside;
        So on a mad horse
        They all of them got,
    And madly away did ride."

SAGACIOUS Goose! Fresh wonders yet!
What spell had power to help you get
Those seven-leagued spectacles, that see
Down to the nineteenth century?

" The mad world, and his madder wife!"
That, in your earlier time of life, —

Though quite demented now, 't is plain, —
Were sober, grave, and almost sane!

And all the tribes, a motley brood
Sprung into being since the flood,
With their hereditary bent
To cerebral bewilderment!

If some old ghost, precise and slow,
Who died a hundred years ago, —
Always supposing he himself
Has lain, meanwhile, upon the shelf, —

Things as they are might only see,
Surely his inference would be
A simultaneous bursting out
Of lunacy the earth about.

" The world is mad; his wife is mad;
  The rising generation 's madder ";
And when a charter can be had,
  Up to the moon they 'll build a ladder !

They caught a horse awhile ago, —
They called him Steam, — but he was slow ;
After the lightning then they ran,
Caught him, — and now they drive the
  span !

THE BIG SHOE.

" There was an old woman
  Who lived in a shoe;
She had so many children
  She did n't know what to **do**:
To some she gave broth,
  And to some she gave bread,
And some she whipped soundly,
  And sent them to bed."

Do you find out the likeness?
  A portly old Dame,—
The mother of millions,—
  Britannia by name:

5

And — howe'er it may strike you
   In reading the song —
Not stinted in space
   For bestowing the throng;
Since the Sun can himself
   Hardly manage to go,
In a day and a night,
   From the heel to the toe.

On the arch of the instep
   She builds up her throne,
And, with seas rolling under,
   She sits there alone;
With her heel at the foot
   Of the Himmalehs planted,
And her toe in the icebergs,
   Unchilled and undaunted.

Yet though justly of all
  Her fine family proud,
'Tis no light undertaking
  To rule such a crowd;
Not to mention the trouble
  Of seeing them fed,
And dispensing with justice
  The broth and the bread.
Some will seize upon one,—
  Some are left with the other,—
And so the whole household
  Gets into a pother.
But the rigid old Dame
  Has a summary way
Of her own, when she finds
  There is mischief to pay.
She just takes up the rod,
  As she lays down the spoon,

And makes their rebellious backs
    Tingle right soon :
Then she bids them, while yet
    The sore smarting they feel,
To lie down, and go to sleep,
    Under her heel !

Only once was she posed, —
    When the little boy Sam,
Who had always before
    Been as meek as a lamb,
Refused to take tea,
    As his mother had bid,
And returned saucy answers
    Because he was chid.

Not content even then,
    He cut loose from the throne,

And set about making
　A shoe of his own;
Which succeeded so well,
　And was filled up so fast,
That the world, in amazement,
　Confessed, at the last, —
Looking on at the work
　With a gasp and a stare, —
That 't was hard to tell which
　Would be best of the pair.

Side by side they are standing
　Together to-day;
Side by side may they keep
　Their strong foothold for aye:
And beneath the broad sea,
　Whose blue depths intervene,
May the finishing string
　Lie unbroken between!

VICTUALS AND DRINK.

"There once was a woman,
   And what do you think?
She lived upon nothing
   But victuals and drink.
Victuals and drink
   Were the chief of her diet,
And yet this poor woman
   Scarce ever was quiet."

AND were you so foolish
   As really to think
That all she could want
   Was her victuals and drink?

And that while she was furnished
  With that sort of diet,
Her feeling and fancy
  Would starve, and be quiet?

Mother Goose knew far better;
  But thought it sufficient
To give a mere hint
  That the fare was deficient;
For I do not believe
  She could ever have meant
To imply there was reason
  For being content.

Yet the mass of mankind
  Is uncommonly slow
To acknowledge the fact
  It behooves them to know;

Or to learn that a woman
  Is not like a mouse,
Needing nothing but cheese,
  And the walls of a house.

But just take a man, —
  Shut him up for a day;
Get his hat and his cane, —
  Put them snugly away;
Give him stockings to mend,
  And three sumptuous meals; —
And then ask him, at night,
  If you dare, how he feels!
Do you think he will quietly
  Stick to the stocking,
While you read the news,
  And " don't care about talking "?

O, many a woman
    Goes starving, I ween,
Who lives in a palace,
    And fares like a queen;
Till the famishing heart,
    And the feverish brain,
Have spelled out to life's end
    The long lesson of pain.

Yet, stay!   To my mind
    An uneasy suggestion
Comes up, that there may be
    Two sides to the question.
That, while here and there proving
    Inflicted privation,
The verdict must often be
    " Wilful starvation."

Since there are men and women
　　Would force one to think
They chose to live only
　　On victuals and drink.

O restless, and craving,
　　Unsatisfied hearts,
Whence never the vulture
　　Of hunger departs!
How long on the husks
　　Of your life will ye feed,
Ignoring the soul,
　　And her famishing need?

Bethink you, when lulled
　　In your shallow content,
T was to Lazarus only
　　The angels were sent;

And 't is he to whose lips
　But earth's ashes are given,
For whom the full banquet
　Is gathered in heaven!

COBWEBS AND BROOMS.

"There was an old woman
  Tossed up in a blanket,
Seventeen times as high as the moon;
  What she did there
  I cannot tell you,
But in her hand she carried a broom.
  Old woman, old woman,
  Old woman, said I,
O whither, O whither, O whither so high?
  To sweep the cobwebs
  Off the sky,
And I'll be back again, by and by."

MIND you, she wore no *wings*,
That she might truly *soar*; no time was lost

In growing such unnecessary things;
But blindly, in a blanket, she was *tost!*

Spasmodically, too!
'T was not enough that she should reach
the moon;
But seventeen times the distance she must
do,
Lest, peradventure, she get back too
soon.

That emblematic broom!
Besom of mad Reform, uplifted high,
That, to reach cobwebs, would precipitate
doom,
And sweep down thunderbolts from out
the sky!

Doubtless, no rubbish lay

About her door, — no work was there to

    do, —

That through the astonished aisles of Night

    and Day,

She took her valorous flight in quest of

    new!

Lo! at her little broom

The great stars laugh, as on their wheels

    of fire

They go, dispersing the eternal gloom,

    And shake Time's dust from off each

    blazing tire!

BLACK SPIDERS.

―――――

" Little Miss Muffet
Sat on a tuffet,
Eating curds and whey :
There came a black spider,
And sat down beside her,
And frightened Miss Muffet away."

To all mortal blisses,
From comfits to kisses,
There 's sure to be something by way of
alloy ;
Each new expectation
Brings fresh aggravation,
And a doubtful amalgam 's the best of our
joy.

You may sit on your tuffet;

Yes, — cushion and stuff it ;

And provide what you please, if you don't
    fancy whey ;

But before you can eat it,

There 'll be — I repeat it —

Some sort of black spider to come in the
    way.

DAFFY–DOWN–DILLY.

————

"Daffy-down-dilly

Is new come to town,

With a petticoat green,

And a bright yellow gown,

And her little white blossoms

Are peeping around."

Now don't you call this

A most exquisite thing?

Don't it give you a thrill

With the thought of the spring,

Such as once, in your childhood,

You felt, when you found

The first yellow buttercups
　　Spangling the ground?

When the lilac was fresh
　　With its glory of leaves,
And the swallows came fluttering
　　Under the eaves?
When the bluebird flashed by
　　Like a magical thing,
And you looked for a fairy
　　Astride of his wing?

When the clear, running water,
　　Like tinkling of bells,
Bore along the bare roadside
　　A song of the dells, —
And the mornings were fresh
　　With unfailing delight,

While the sweet summer hush
  Always came with the night?

O daffy-down-dilly,
  With robings of gold!
As our hearts every year
  To your coming unfold,
And sweet memories stir
  Through the hardening mould,
We feel how earth's blossomings
  Surely are given
To keep the soul fresh
  For the spring-time of heaven!

BAA, BAA, BLACK SHEEP!

———

" Baa, baa, black sheep!
Have you any wool?
Yes, sir, — no, sir, —
Three bags full.
One for my master,
One for my dame,
And one for the little boy
That lives in the lane."

'T is the same question as of old;
And still the doubter saith,
" Can any good be made to come
From out of Nazareth?"

No sheep so black in all the flock,—
    No human heart so bare,—
But hath some warm and generous stock
    Of kindliness to share.

It may be treasured secretly
    For dear ones at the hearth;
Or be bestowed by stealth along
    The by-ways of the earth;—

And though no searching eye may see,
    Nor busy tongue may tell,
Perchance, where largest love is laid,
    The Master knoweth well!

THE TWISTER.

"A twister, in twisting, would twist him a twist,
And, twisting his twists, seven twists he doth twist;
If one twist, in twisting, untwist from the twist,
The twist, untwisting, untwists the twist."

A RAVELLED rainbow overhead
Lets down to life its varying thread:
Love's blue,—Joy's gold,—and, fair be-
    tween,
Hope's shifting light of emerald green;
With, either side, in deep relief,
A crimson Pain,—a violet Grief.

Wouldst thou, amid their gleaming hues,
Clutch after those, and these refuse?
Believe, — as thy beseeching eyes
Follow their lines, and sound the skies, —
There, where the fadeless glories shine,
An unseen angel twists the twine.

And be thou sure, what tint soe'er
The broken rays beneath may wear,
It needs them all, that, broad and white,
God's love may weave the perfect light!

FANTASY.

"I have a little sister,
  They call her peep, peep;
She wades through the water,
  Deep, deep, deep;
She climbs up the mountains,
  High, high, high;
My poor little sister,
  She has but one eye!"

Rough Common Sense doth here confess
  Her kinship to Imagination;
Betraying also, I should guess,
  Some little pride in the relation.

For even while vexed, and puzzled too,
   By the vagaries of the latter, —
Fearful what next the child may do, —
   She looks with loving wonder at her.

Plain Sense keeps ever to the road
That's beaten down and daily trod;
While Fancy fords the rivers wide,
And scrambles up the mountain-side:
By which exploits she's always getting
Either a tumble or a wetting.

While simple Sense looks straight before,
Fancy "peeps" further, and sees more;
And yet, if left to walk alone,
   May chance, like most long-sighted people,
To trip her foot against a stone
   While gazing at a distant steeple.

Nay, worse! with all her grace erratic,
And feats aerial and aquatic,
Her flights sublime, and moods ecstatic,
She of the vision wild and high
Hath but a solitary eye!
And, — not to quote the Scripture, which
Forebodes the falling in the ditch, —
Doubtless by following such a guide
Blindly, in all her wanderings wide,
The world, at best, would get o' one side.

What then?   To rid us of our doubt
    Is there no other thing to do
But we must turn poor Fancy out,
    And only downright Fact pursue?

Ah, see you not, bewildered man!
The heavenly beauty of the plan?

'T was so ordained, in counsels high,
   To give to sweet Imagination
A single deep and glorious eye;
   But then 't was meant, in compensation,
That Common Sense, with optics keen, —
As maid of honor to a queen, —
On her blind side should always stay,
And keep her in the middle way.

JINGLING AND JANGLING.

"Little Jack Jingle
Used to live single.
But when he got tired
Of that kind of life,
He left off being single,
And lived with his wife."

Your period's pointed, most excellent Mother!

Pray what did he do when he tired of the other?

For a man so deplorably prone to ennui

But a queer sort of husband is likely to be.

The fatigue might recur, — and, in case it
should be so,

Why not take a wife on a limited lease, O ?

Grant the privilege, pray, to his idiosyn-
crasy, —

Some natures won't bear to be too closely
pinned, you see, —

And, at worst, the poor Benedict might
advertise,

When weary, at length, of the light of his
eyes, —

Or failing to find her, it may be, in salt, —

"Disposed of, indeed, for no manner of
fault,"

(To borrow a figure of speech from the
mart,)

"But because the late owner has taken a
start!"

I believe once before you have cautiously
    said

Something quite as concise on this delicate
    head,

When distantly hinting at "needles and
    pins,"

And that "when a man marries, his trouble
    begins";

But I don't recollect that you ever pretend

To prophesy anything as to the *end*.

Unless we may learn it of Peter, — the
    bumpkin,

Renowned for naught else but his eating
    of pumpkin;

Whose wife — I don't see how he happened
    to get her —

Had a taste, very likely, for things that
    were better:

Since, fearing to lose her, at last it be-
fell

He bethought him of shutting her up in a
shell;

By which brilliant contrivance she *kept* very
well!

What he did with her next, the tradition
don't say,

But she seems to be somehow got out of
the way,

For the ill-fated Peter was wedded once
more,

To find his bewilderment worse than before;

If the first for her spouse had but small
predilection,

Now 't was his turn, alas! to fall short in
affection.

And how do you think that he conquered
the evil?

Why, simply by *lifting himself to her level;*

By leaving his pumpkins, and learning to
spell,

He came, saith the story, to love her right
well;

And the mythical memoir its moral con-
trives

For the lasting instruction of husbands
and wives.

THE OLD WOMAN OF SURREY.

"There was an old woman in Surrey,
  Who was morn, noon, and night in a hurry;
    Called her husband a fool,
    Drove the children to school,
  The worrying old woman of Surrey."

'T was an ancient earldom over the sea,
And it must be now as it used to be;
Yet the sketch is of one I have known
      before, —
The very old woman that lives next door.

7

One thing is unquestionable,—she 's
    " smart,"—
As they say of an apple that 's rather tart;
For her nearest friends, I think, would
    allow her
To be, at her best, but a " pleasant sour."

There 's a certain electrical atmosphere
That you feel beforehand, when she 's near:
And—unless you 've a wonderful deal of
    pluck—
A shrinking fear that you might be
    " struck."

She moves with such a bustle and rush,—
Such an elemental stir and crush,
As makes the branches bend and fall
In the breeze that blows up a thunder-squall.

And yet, it is only her endless " hurry ";
She 's not so bad if she would n't " worry,"
And, for all the worlds that she has to make,
If the six days' time she 'd only take.

You may talk about Surrey, or Devon, or
     Kent,
But I doubt if a special location was meant;
It may sound severe, — but it seems to me
That a " representative " woman was she ;

And that here and there you may chance
     to trace
Some specimens extant of the race :
For a slip of the stock, as I 've a notion,
Somehow " in the Mayflower " crossed the
     ocean.

PICKLE PEPPERS.

"Peter Piper picked a peck of pickle peppers;
 And a peck of pickle peppers Peter Piper picked;
If Peter Piper picked a peck of pickle peppers
 Where's the peck of pickle peppers Peter Piper
 picked?"

Poor Peter toiled his life away,
That afterward the world might say
"Where is the peck of peppers he
Did gather so industriously?"
The peppers are embalmed in metre, —
But who, alas! inquires for Peter?

In sun or storm, by night and day,

Scant time for sleep, and none for play,

Still the poor fool did nothing reck,

If only he might pick his peck:

And what result from all hath sprung,

But just to bite somebody's tongue?

Or, — Lady Fortune playing fickle, —

Get some one in a precious pickle?

HUMPTY DUMPTY.

"Humpty Dumpty sat on a wall:
Humpty Dumpty had a great fall:
Not all the king's horses nor all the king's men
Could set Humpty Dumpty up again."

FULL many a project that never was hatched
Falls down, and gets shattered beyond be-
    ing patched;
And luckily, too! for if all came to chick-
    ens,
Then things without feathers might go to
    the dickens.

If each restless unit that moves among men
Might climb to a place with the privileged
    " ten,"
Pray tell us where all the commotion would
    stop !
Must the whole pan of milk, forsooth, rise
    to the top ?

If always the statesman attained to his hopes,
And grasped the great helm, who would
    stand by the ropes?
Or if all dainty fingers their duties might
    choose,
Who would wash up the dishes, and polish
    the shoes ?

Suppose every aspirant writing a book
Contrived to get published, by hook or by
    crook ;

Geologists then of a later creation

Would be startled, I fancy, to find a forma-
tion

Proving how the poor world did most wo-
fully sink

Beneath mountains of paper, and oceans of
ink !

Or even suppose all the women were married ;

By whom would superfluous babies be carried ?

Where would be the good aunts that should
knit all the stockings ?

Or nurses, to do up the singings and rock-
ings ?

Wise spinsters, to lay down their wonderful
rules,

And with theories rare to enlighten the
    fools, —
Or to look after orphans, and primary
    schools?

No! Failure's a part of the infinite plan;
Who finds that he can't, must give way to
    who can;
And as one and another drops out of the
    race,
Each stumbles at last to his suitable place.

So the great scheme works on, — though,
    like eggs from the wall,
Little single designs to such ruin may fall,
That not all the world's might, of its horses
    or men,
Could set their crushed hopes at the sum-
    mit again.

SUNDAY AND MONDAY.

———

"As Tommy Snooks and Bessy Brooks
  Were walking out one Sunday,
Says Tommy Snooks to Bessy Brooks,
  To-morrow will be Monday."

No doubt you are smiling at such a remark,

And thinking poor Snooks but a pitiful
    spark;

But the words have a meaning, worth look-
    ing for, too,

As I'll presently try and demonstrate for
    you.

'T was a pity, indeed, in that moment of
  leisure,
To dampen poor Bessy's hebdomadal pleas-
  ure,
Suggesting that close on the beautiful Sunday
Must come all the common-place horrors
  of Monday;

That he to his toiling, and she to her
  tub,
Must turn, and take up with another week's
  rub;
Yet a truth for us all, since the shade of
  the real
Follows fast on the track of each sunny
  ideal.

Now and then we may pause on Life's
    pleasant oases;

But between lie the desert's grim, desolate
    spaces;

And our feet, with all patience, must trav-
    erse them still,

Reaching forward to blessing, through
    bearing of ill.

Yet for Snooks and his Bessy, — for me
    and for you, —

Comes a Saturday night when the wage
    will be due;

And we'll say to each other, in ecstasy,
    one day,

"To-morrow — the endless to-morrow — is
    Sunday!"

CONCLUSION.

Doubtless I might go on to quote,
With added paraphrase and note,
Enough of rhymes to fill a scroll,
That, bundled up, should be a roll
As bulky as a broad-brimmed hat;
But " verbum sapienti sat!"
Suffice it to have struck the vein,
    And shown some specimens of ore;
If any seek for further gain,
    The mine still holds abundance more.
A mental pickaxe and a biggin
Are all you need to go to diggin'.

For, as the Swedish seer contends,
All things comprise an inner sense ;
There 's nothing we can write or say,
In howsoever simple way,
But seems a body, built to hide
The soul, that straightway is supplied ;
And many a fool, and prophet too,
Hath spoken wiser than he knew.

One parting word, and I am gone :
  If I 've prevailed to make you see
  These things as they appear to me,
Then have I proved my Goose a Swan ;
And I, descended of her line,
  And bearing yet the ancient name,
May, for this ancestress of mine,
  Claim place upon the page of fame ; —
That not a bard of Saxon tongue
More true to nature ever sung ;

More surely soothed, more deeply taught,
Or passing fact more keenly caught;
And that — exalted side by side
With him of Avon, in the pride
And love of millions — we should lay
The tribute at her feet to-day
That owns her, in this latter age,
Goose, truly, — but, in savor, Sage!

THE END.

CATALOGUE

OF THE

PUBLICATIONS

OF

RUDD & CARLETON,

130 GRAND STREET,

(BROOKS BUILDING, COR. OF BROADWAY,)

NEW YORK.

NEW BOOKS
And New Editions Just Published by
RUDD & CARLETON,
130 Grand Street,
NEW YORK (BROOKS BUILDING, COR. OF BROADWAY.)

NOTHING TO WEAR.

A Satirical Poem. By WILLIAM ALLEN BUTLER. Profusely and elegantly embellished with fine Illustrations on tinted paper, by Hoppin. Muslin, price 50 cents.

MILES STANDISH ILLUSTRATED.

With exquisite *Photographs* from original Drawings by JOHN W. EHNINGER, illustrating Longfellow's new Poem. Bound in elegant quarto, morocco covers, price $6 00

BOOK OF THE CHESS CONGRESS.

A complete History of Chess in America and Europe, with Morphy's best games. By D. W. FISKE, editor of *Chess Monthly* (assisted by Morphy and Paulsen). Price $1 50.

WOMAN'S THOUGHTS ABOUT WOMEN.

The latest and best work by the author of "John Halifax, Gentleman," "Agatha's Husband," "The Ogilvies," &c. From the London edition. Muslin, price $1 00.

VERNON GROVE;

By Mrs. Caroline H. Glover. "A Novel which will give its author high rank among the novelists of the day."—*Atlantic Monthly.* 12mo., Muslin, price $1 00

BALLAD OF BABIE BELL,

And other Poems. By Thomas Bailey Aldrich. The first selected collection of verses by this author. 12mo Exquisitely printed, and bound in muslin, price 75 cents.

TRUE LOVE NEVER DID RUN SMOOTH.

An Eastern Tale, in Verse. By Thomas Bailey Aldrich, author of "Babie Bell, and other Poems." Printed on colored plate paper. Muslin, price 50 cents

BEATRICE CENCI.

A Historical Novel. By F. D. Guerrazzi. Translated from the original Italian by Luigi Monti. Muslin, two volumes in one, with steel portrait price $1 25.

ISABELLA ORSINI.

A new historical novel. By F. D. Guerrazzi, author of "Beatrice Cenci." Translated by Monti, of Harvard College. With steel portrait. Muslin, price $1 25.

DOCTOR ANTONIO.

A charming Love Tale of Italy. By G. Ruffini, author of "Lorenzo Benoni," "Dear Experience," &c From the last London edition. Muslin, price $1 00.

DEAR EXPERIENCE.

A Tale. By G. Ruffini, author of "Doctor Antonio," "Lorenzo Benoni," &c. With illustrations by Leech, *of the London Punch.* 12mo. Muslin. price $1 00

LECTURES OF LOLA MONTEZ.

Including her " Autobiography," " Wits and Women of Paris," " Comic Aspect of Love," " Gallantry," &c. A new edition, large 12mo. Muslin, price $1 25.

EDGAR POE AND HIS CRITICS.

By Mrs. SARAH HELEN WHITMAN. A volume possessing many attractions and which has created considerable interest among the *literati*. 12mo. Muslin, price 75 cts

THE GREAT TRIBULATION;

Or Things coming on the Earth. By Rev. JOHN CUMMING, D.D., author of " Apocalyptic Sketches," &c. From the English edition. FIRST SERIES. Muslin, price $1 00.

THE GREAT TRIBULATION.

SECOND SERIES of the new work by Rev. DR. CUMMING, which has awakened such an excitement throughout the religious community. 12mo. Muslin, price $1 00.

ADVENTURES OF VERDANT GREEN.

By CUTHBERT BEDE, B.A. The best humorous story of College Life ever published. *80th edition*, from English plates. Nearly 200 original illustrations, price $1 00.

CURIOSITIES OF NATURAL HISTORY.

By FRANCIS T. BUCKLAND, M.A. A sparkling collection of surprises in Natural History, and the charm of a lively narrative. From 4th London edition, price $1 25.

BROWN'S CARPENTER'S ASSISTANT.

The best practical work on Architecture ; with Plans for every description of Building. Illustrated with over 200 Plates. Strongly bound in leather, price $5 00.

THE VAGABOND.

A volume of Miscellaneous Papers, treating in colloquia sketches upon Literature, Society, and Art. By ADAM BADEAU. Bound in muslin, 12mo, price $1 00.

ALEXANDER VON HUMBOLDT.

A new and popular Biography of this celebrated *Savant,* including his travels and labors, with an introduction by BAYARD TAYLOR. One vol., steel portrait, price $1 25.

LOVE (L'AMOUR).

By M. JULES MICHELET. Author of "A History of France," &c. Translated from the French by J. W. Pa'mer, M.D. One vol., 12mo. Muslin, price $1 00.

WOMAN (LA FEMME).

A sequel and companion to "Love" (L'Amour) by the same author, MICHELET. Translated from the French by Dr. J. W. Palmer. 12mo. Muslin, price $1 00.

LIFE OF HUGH MILLER.

Author of "Schools and Schoolmasters," "Old Red Sandstone," &c. Reprinted from the English edition. One large 12mo. Muslin, new edition, price $1 25.

AFTERNOON OF UNMARRIED LIFE.

An interesting theme admirably treated. Companion to Miss Muloch's "Woman's Thoughts about Women." From London edition. 12mo. Muslin, price, $1 00.

SOUTHWOLD.

By MRS. LILLIE DEVEREUX UMSTED. "A spirited an well drawn Society novel—somewhat intensified but bold and clever." 12mo. Muslin, price $1 00.

DOESTICKS' LETTERS.

Being a compilation of the Original Letters of O. K. P
Doesticks, P. B. With many comic tinted illustrations
by John McLenan. 12mo. Muslin. price $1 00

PLU-RI-BUS-TAH.

A song that's by-no-author. *Not* a parody on "Hia-
watha." By Doesticks. With 150 humorous illustrations by McLenan. 12mo. Muslin, price $1 00

THE ELEPHANT CLUB.

An irresistibly droll volume. By Doesticks, assisted by
Knight Russ Ockside, M.D. One of his best works
Profusely illustrated by McLenan. Muslin, price $1 00.

THE WITCHES OF NEW YORK.

A new humorous work by Doesticks; being minute,
particular, and faithful Revelations of Black Art
Mysteries in Gotham. 12mo. Muslin, price $1 00

TWO WAYS TO WEDLOCK.

A Novellette. Reprinted from the columns of Morris &
Willis' *New York Home Journal.* 12mo. Hand-
somely bound in muslin. Price $ 00,

HAMMOND'S POLITICAL HISTORY.

A History of Political Parties in the State of New York.
By Jabez B. Hammond, L.L.D. 3 vols., octavo, with steel
portraits of all the Governors. Muslin. Price, $6 00.

ROMANCE OF A POOR YOUNG MAN.

From the French of Octave Feuillet. An admirable
and striking work of fiction. Translated from the
Seventh Paris edition. 12mo. Muslin, price $1 00

THE CULPRIT FAY.

By JOSEPH RODMAN DRAKE. A charming edition of this world-celebrated Faery Poem. Printed on colored plate paper. Muslin, 12mo. Frontispiece. Price, 50 cts.

THE NEW AND THE OLD;

Or, California and India in Romantic Aspects. By J. W. PALMER, M.D., author of "Up and Down the Irrawaddi." Abundantly illustrated. Muslin, 12mo. $1,25.

UP AND DOWN THE IRRAWADDI;

Or, the Golden Dagon. Being passages of adventure in the Burman Empire. By J. W. PALMER, M.D., author of "The New and the Old." Illustrated. Price, $1,00.

THE HABITS OF GOOD SOCIETY.

An interesting handbook for Ladies and Gentlemen; with thoughts, hints, and anecdotes, concerning social observances, taste, and good manners. Muslin, price $1 25.

RECOLLECTIONS OF THE REVOLUTION.

A private manuscript journal of home events, kept during the American Revolution by the Daughter of a Clergyman. Printed in unique style. Muslin. Price, $1,00

HARTLEY NORMAN.

A New Novel. "Close and accurate observation, enables the author to present the scenes of everyday life with great spirit and originality." Muslin, 12mo. Price, $1,25.

MOTHER GOOSE FOR GROWN FOLKS.

An unique and attractive little Holiday volume. Printed on tinted paper, with frontispiece by Billings. 12mo. Elegantly bound in fancy colored muslin, price 75 cts.